DREAM DOODLE DRAW!
Awesome Adventures

Under the Sea • **Castles and Kingdoms** • **Farm Friends**

LITTLE SIMON

New York London Toronto Sydney New Delhi

The doodles in this book were created by

_____

LITTLE SIMON

An imprint of Simon & Schuster Children's Publishing Division

1230 Avenue of the Americas, New York, New York 10020

First Little Simon bind-up edition May 2016

Under the Sea and *Castles and Kingdoms* copyright © 2014 by Simon & Schuster, Inc.

Farm Friends copyright © 2015 by Simon & Schuster, Inc.

All rights reserved, including the right of reproduction in whole or in part in any form.

LITTLE SIMON is a registered trademark of Simon & Schuster, Inc., and associated colophon is a trademark of Simon & Schuster, Inc.

For information about special discounts for bulk purchases, please contact Simon & Schuster Special Sales

at 1-866-506-1949 or business@simonandschuster.com.

The Simon & Schuster Speakers Bureau can bring authors to your live event. For more information or to book an event contact the

Simon & Schuster Speakers Bureau at 1-866-248-3049 or visit our website at www.simonspeakers.com.

Designed by Jay Colvin

Manufactured in China 0816 SCP

2 4 6 8 10 9 7 5 3

ISBN 978-1-4814-6292-1

The contents in this book were previously published individually as *Under the Sea*,

Castles and Kingdoms, and *Farm Friends*.

Get ready to dive in to the world under the sea!

Doodle some faces onto these sea stars!

This orca is dreaming about something yummy.

Draw your favorite treat in his thought bubble!

Decorate these shells with stripes, swirls, and polka dots!

Start

This big blue whale is looking for her baby! Can you help her find him?

Finish

These fish have found an anchor!
Draw the ship that dropped it.

Can you spot these images in the scene?

Color them in!

Ooh! A message in a bottle!

What do you think the message said?
Write it here.

Fill these pages with all kinds of fish!

Two friendly dolphins are bouncing with the waves.

Draw two more on this page!

Connect the dots to complete these
scary deep-sea creatures!
Then color them in!

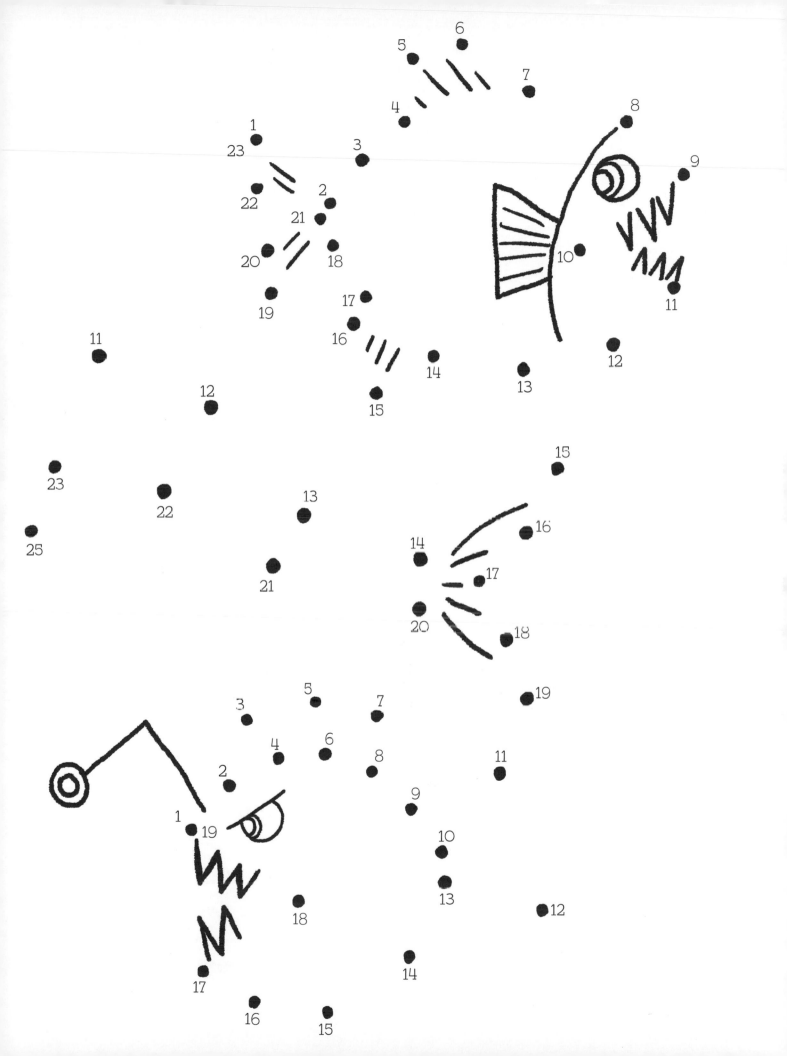

Eek! These waters are filled with eels!

Doodle your own eels on this page.

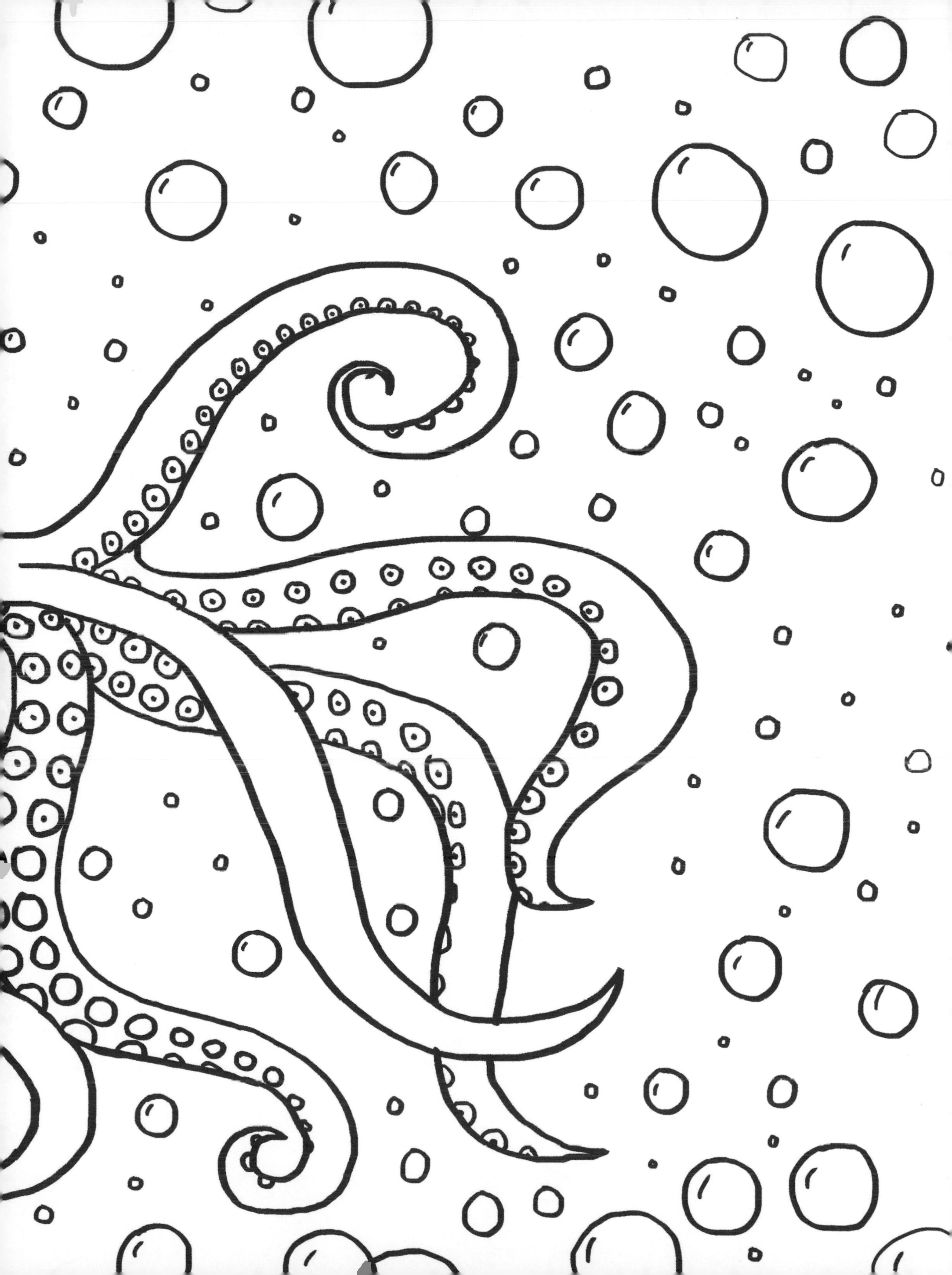

Doodle some patterns onto these turtles' shells!

A submarine is exploring the bottom of the sea.
What does it see?

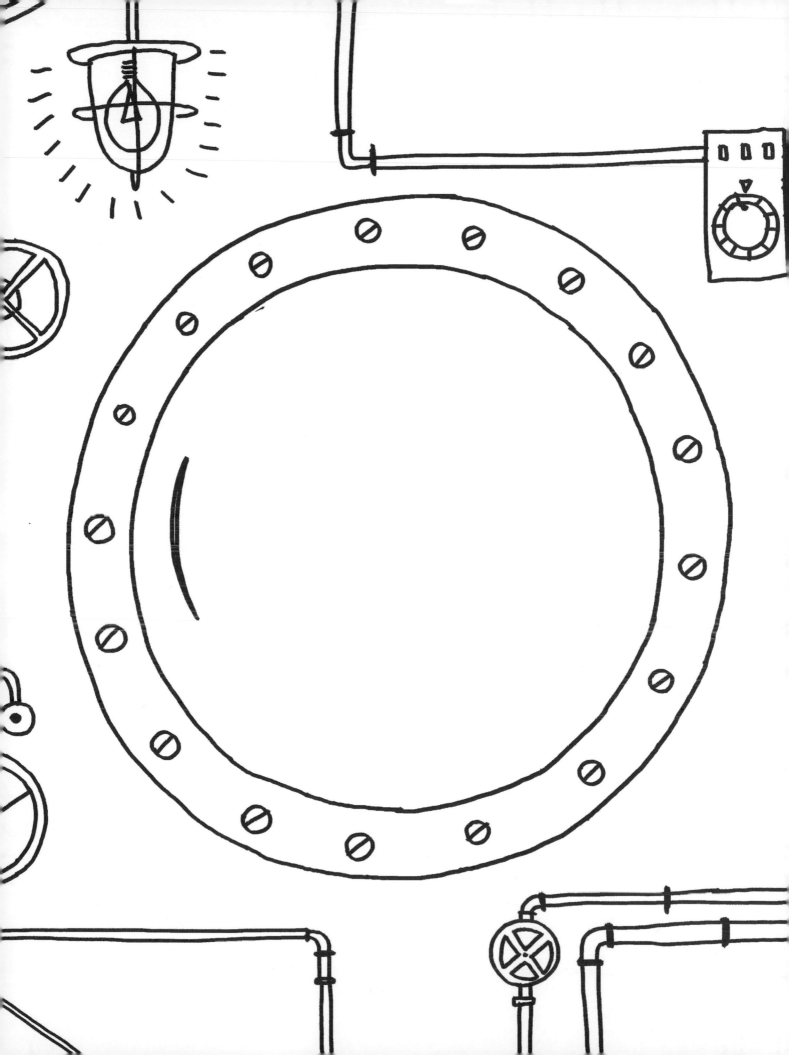

Draw some googly eyes on these crabs!

Yikes! This barracuda is chasing some angelfish.

Draw some rocks between them
to keep the angelfish safe!

These baby turtles are making their way
toward the ocean.

Draw the shoreline so they can see
how far they have to go!

These sea horses are resting on sea grasses and coral.
Use your favorite colors to fill in these pages.

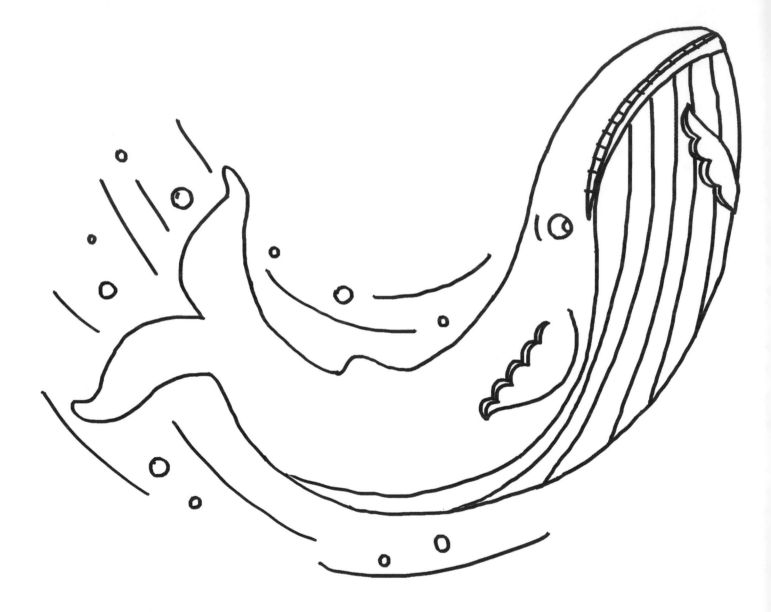

This blue whale is looking for some lunch.

What do you think he wants to eat?
Draw it here.

What is slithering out from under the rocks?
It's an __ __ __ !
Fill up the rest of this page any way you wish!

Color in these sea urchins!

Draw the other half of this octopus!

Connect the dots to create some sea turtles.
Now color them in any way you like!

Draw your own unique fish!

What would you name it? Write the name on the line.

_____

A diver is looking for some buried treasure! Can you help him find it?

Start

Finish

Now fill the treasure chest with jewels!

If you could dream up your own undersea world,
what would it look like?
Draw it for everyone to see!

These two fish are kissing!
Draw a heart made out of bubbles around them!

Can you spot the hammerhead shark? Color it in!

Some creatures are swimming across the ocean floor.
Connect the dots to find out what they are!

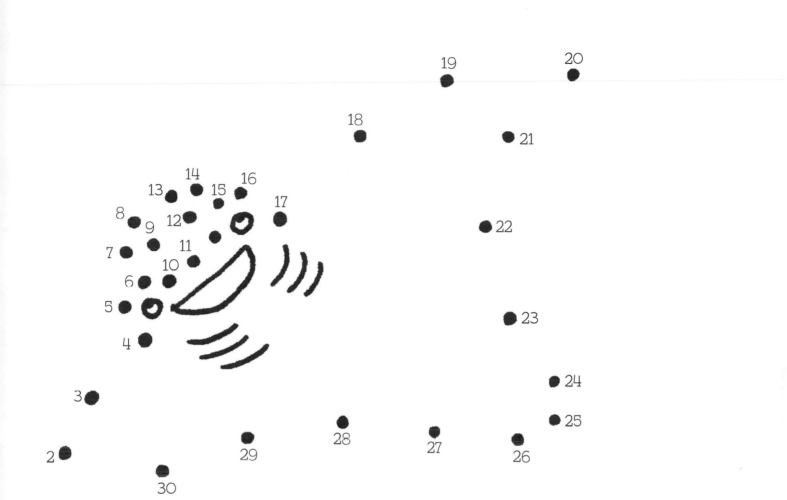

They are manta rays!

These snorkelers are looking for some colorful fish.
Add them to the scene!

Draw what's above and below sea level.

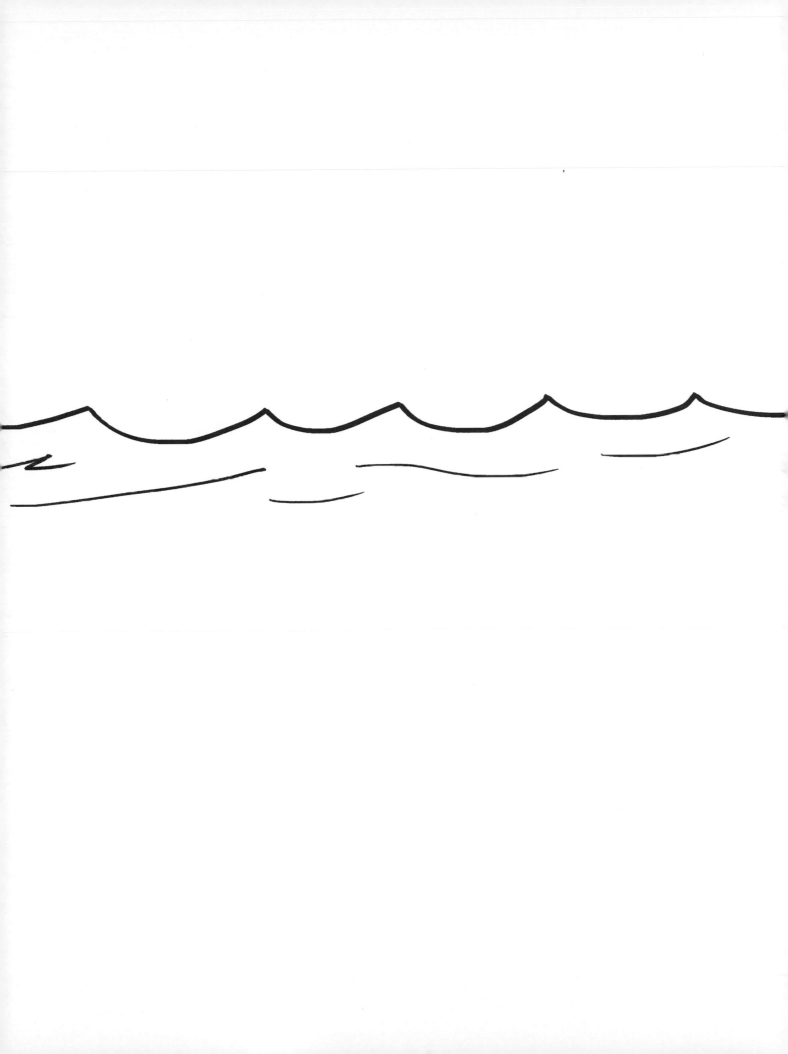

Create your own seashells!

Doodle two silly sea creatures!

Now give them names!

_____ _____

Add some colors and patterns to this coral.

These sea anemones sway back and forth in the water.
Add a few more sea anemones to the scene!

Do you see these objects in this scene?

Color them in!

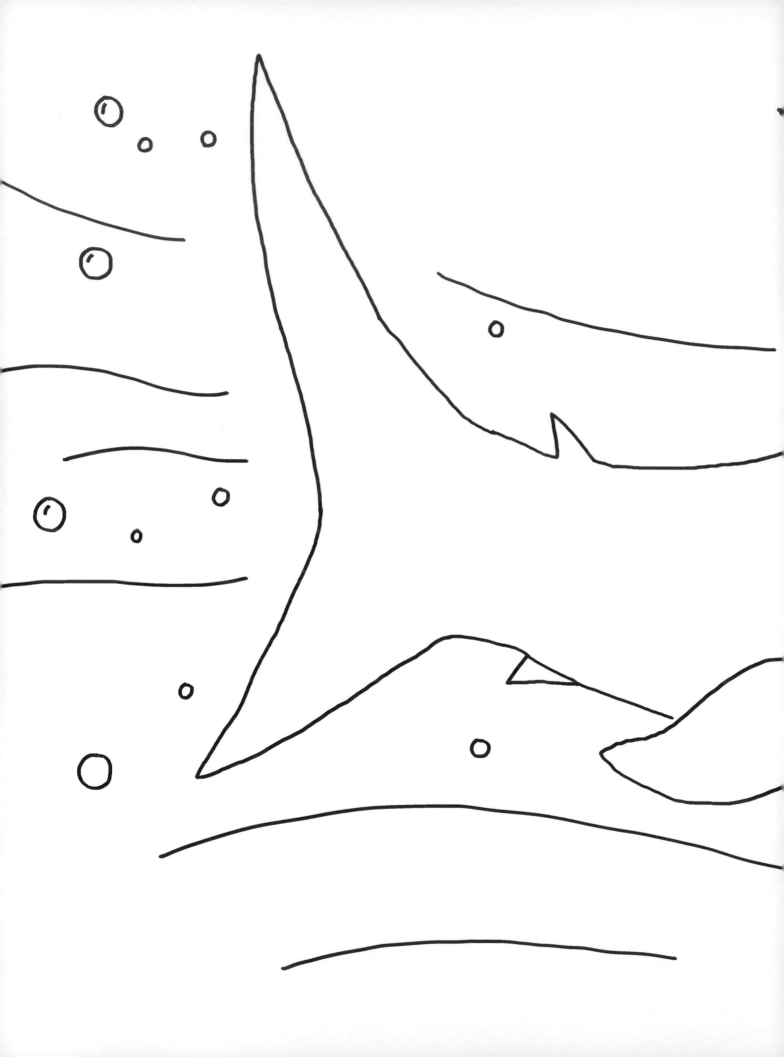

Doodle a pair of cool sunglasses onto this shark!

Connect the dots to give these lobsters some shade!

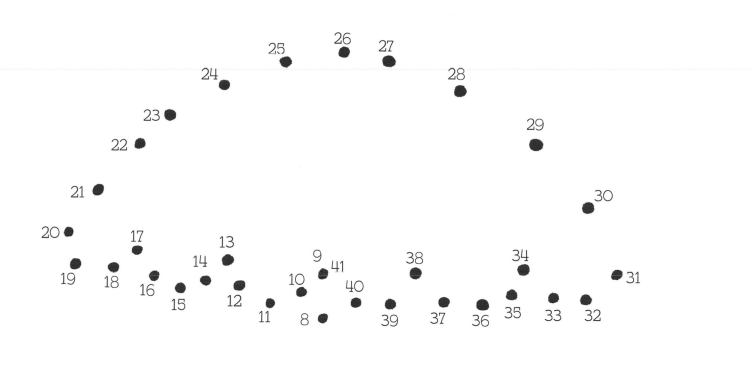

Doodle your favorite sea creatures onto this coral reef.

Give these jellyfish some fancy hats!

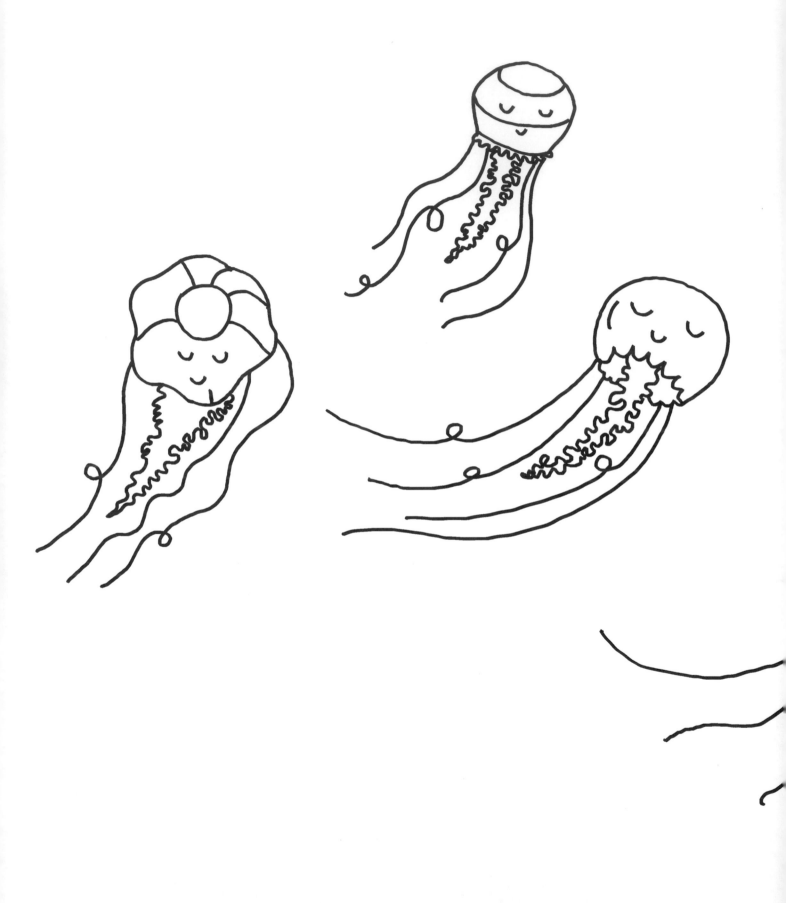

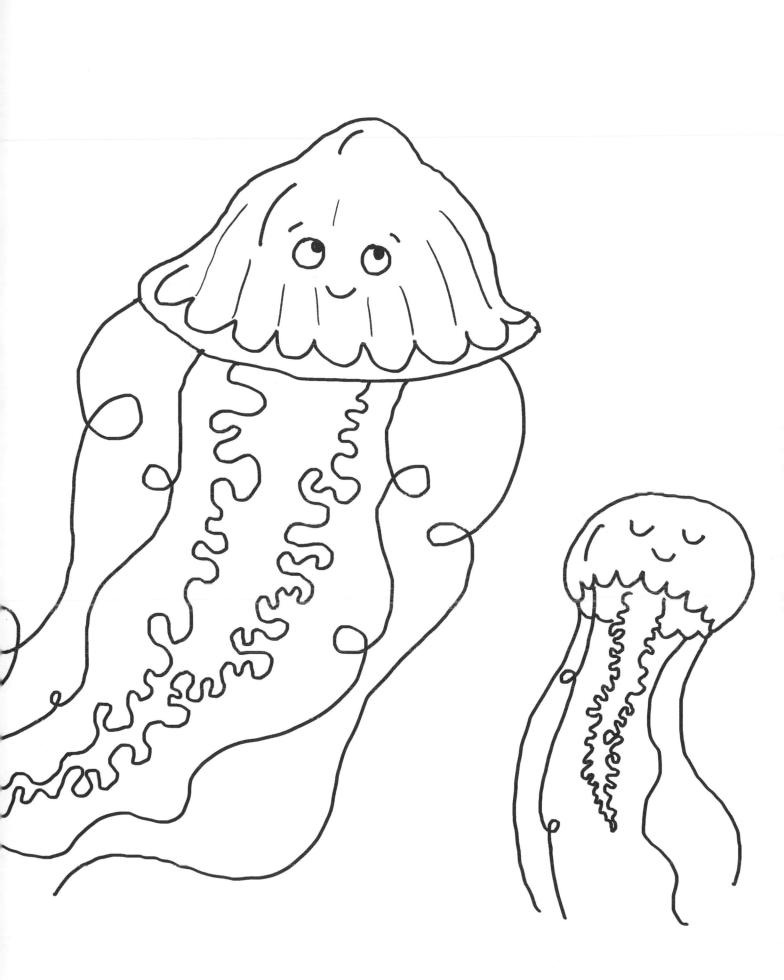

Ooh! Another message in a bottle!

What do you think the message said?
Write it here.

Welcome to the land of castles and kingdoms! Color in this royal scene.

These dragons are flying high in the sky.
Draw more!

Color in this scene!

What's happening inside the palace windows?

Decorate these shields!

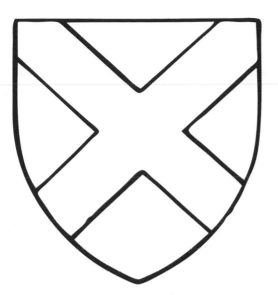

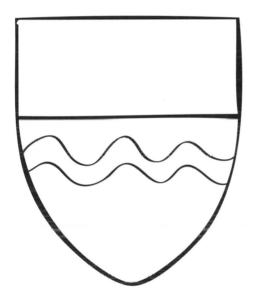

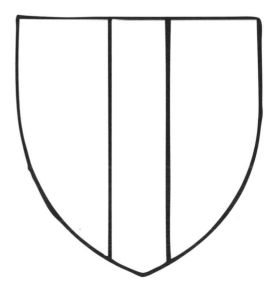

The prince is trying to rescue his princess. Can you help him?

Start

Finish

These people are waiting to enter the castle. Should the drawbridge be up or down? Draw it so they can cross the moat!

Here are a few of the magical creatures in these lands.
Color them in!

Fairy

Gnome

Wizard

Color in these crowns!

Connect the dots to see who—or what—is sitting on this throne.

This prince is practicing his archery.

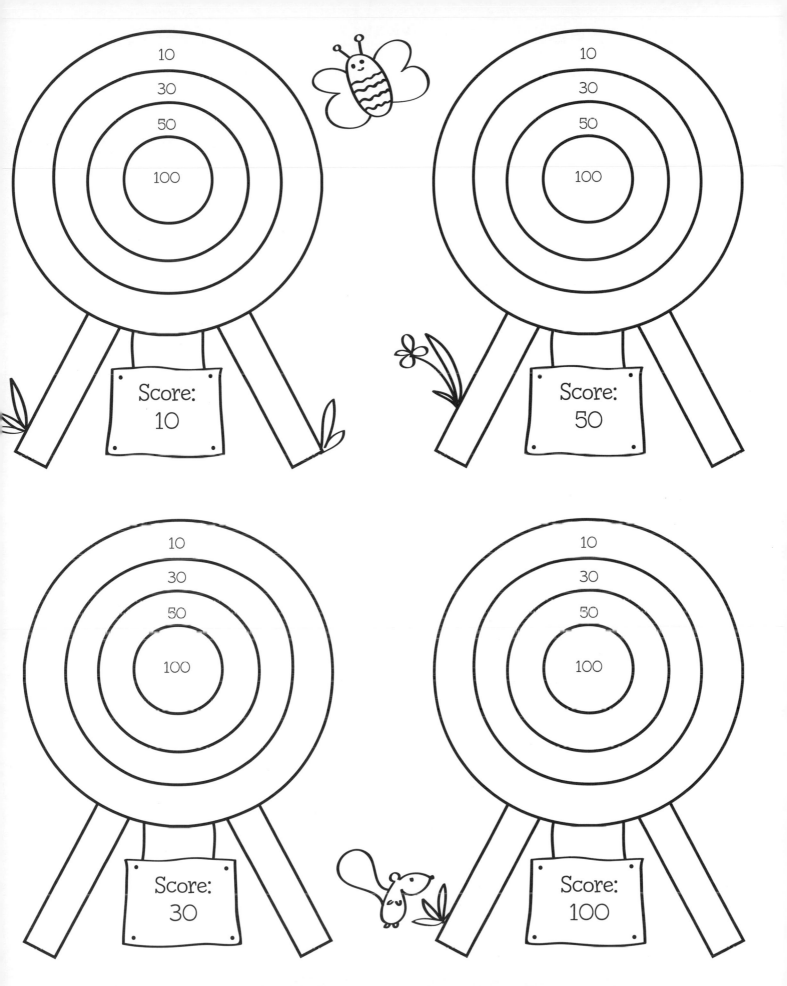

Draw an arrow onto each target according to the score below it.

Yikes! A giant is chasing the princess.

Draw a moat around the princess and the castle to help her get away.

If you could invent your own magical creatures,
what would they look like? Draw them here!

This witch is making a potion. Color in the scene!

These are the ingredients for the witch's potion.
Can you draw each ingredient next to its name?

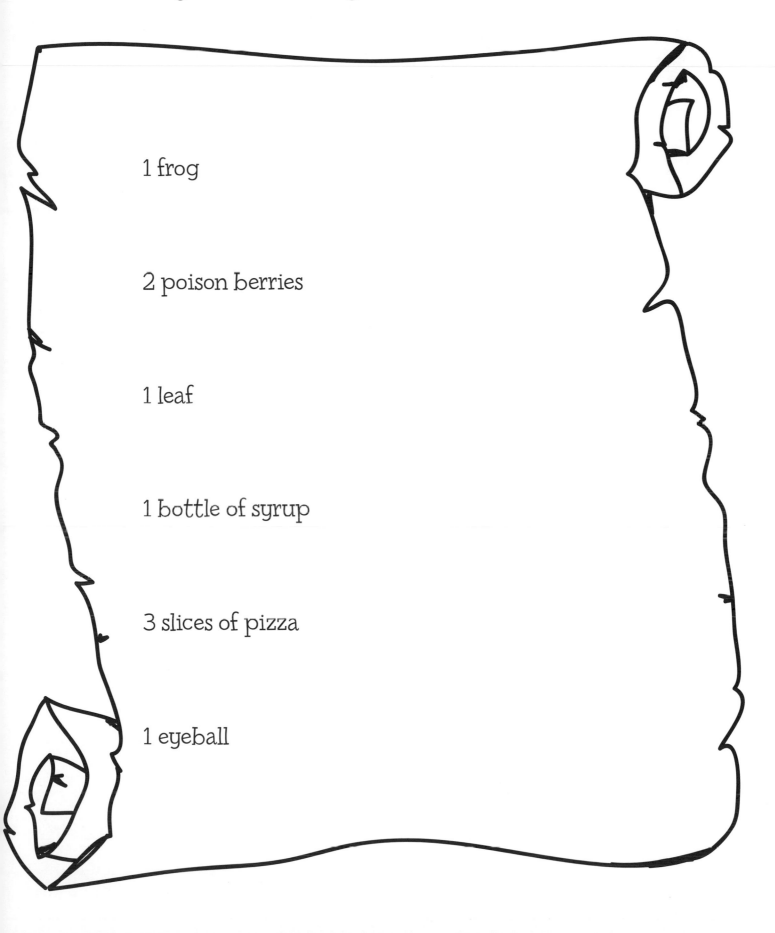

1 frog

2 poison berries

1 leaf

1 bottle of syrup

3 slices of pizza

1 eyeball

It's time for a royal feast.
Draw lots of food on the table that is fit for a king!

Color in this scene.

This princess has one wish. Draw it in her thought bubble!

Draw some fancy designs on these ball gowns fit for a princess!

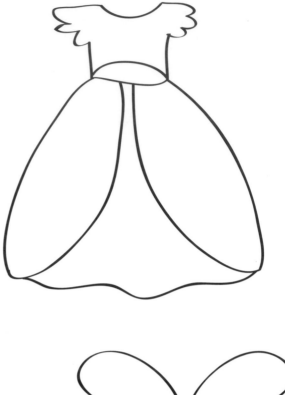

Now add some gemstones and decorations to these tiaras!

The town is bustling with stores and people. Color them in.

There are lots of homes in town. Draw people in the windows.

Now draw some pets in the windows!

The queen needs to get to her horse-drawn carriage. Can you help her?

Start

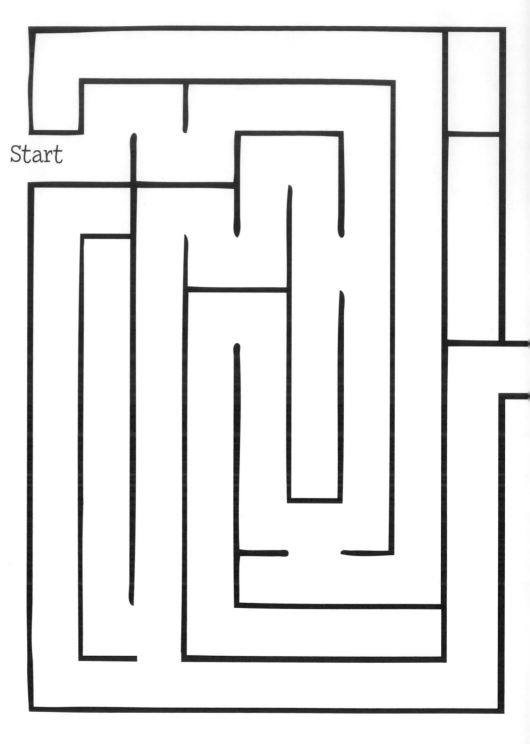

Finish

Color in this royal family crest!

If you had your own family crest, what would it look like?
Draw it here.

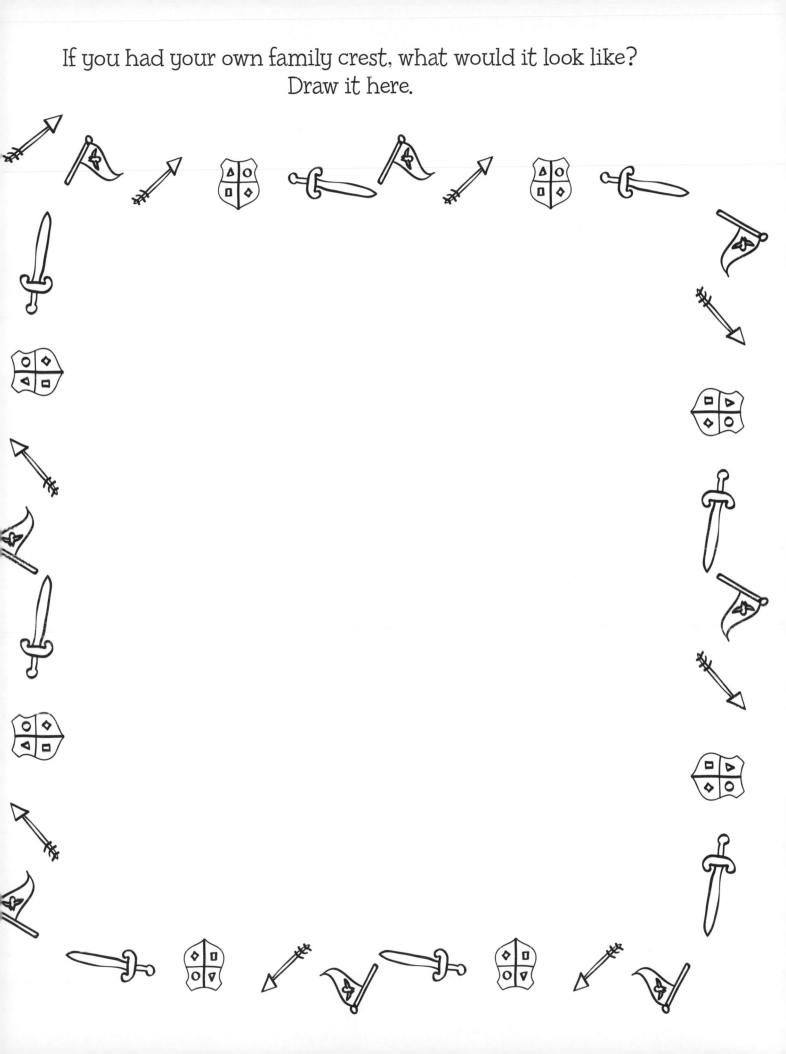

The royal ship is setting out to sea. Draw more people on board!

What's below the ship in the water?
Draw some fish, a whale, and a few more mermaids!

The royal jester is juggling. Color him in!

The royal harp player is performing. Color her in!

Color in the castle's beautiful stained-glass windows.

Color in these different castles.

Now color in the flag for each castle.

The royal garden is filled with fancy flowers and ripe fruit.
Add some more flowers and fruit to the scene!

Color in these gemstones!

This is the princess's royal bedroom.
Color it in and then draw the princess.

This is the prince's royal bedroom.
Color it in and then draw the prince.

The royal pond is filled with lots of creatures. Color in this scene.

Will this frog turn into a prince?
Color it in and then turn the page to find out!

The frog turned into a prince! Color him in.

Now draw a princess.

Can you spot these images in the scene?

These are the royal pets.
Color them in and then name them using the blank line below each pet!

_____

_____

_____

_____

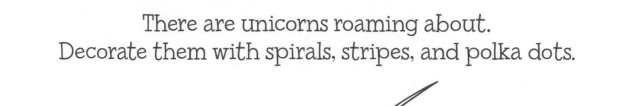

There are unicorns roaming about.
Decorate them with spirals, stripes, and polka dots.

Now decorate the wings of these fairies.

Some of the shops in town have funny names. In the boxes below, can you draw the animal that matches each shop's name?

The Red Rabbit

The Purple Dove

The Gray Dog

THE GOLDEN OX

Draw some fancy designs on these robes fit for a king!

Now add some decorations to these crowns!

There's an archery tournament going on. Draw an arrow onto each of the targets to show who got a bull's-eye. Then color in the scene.

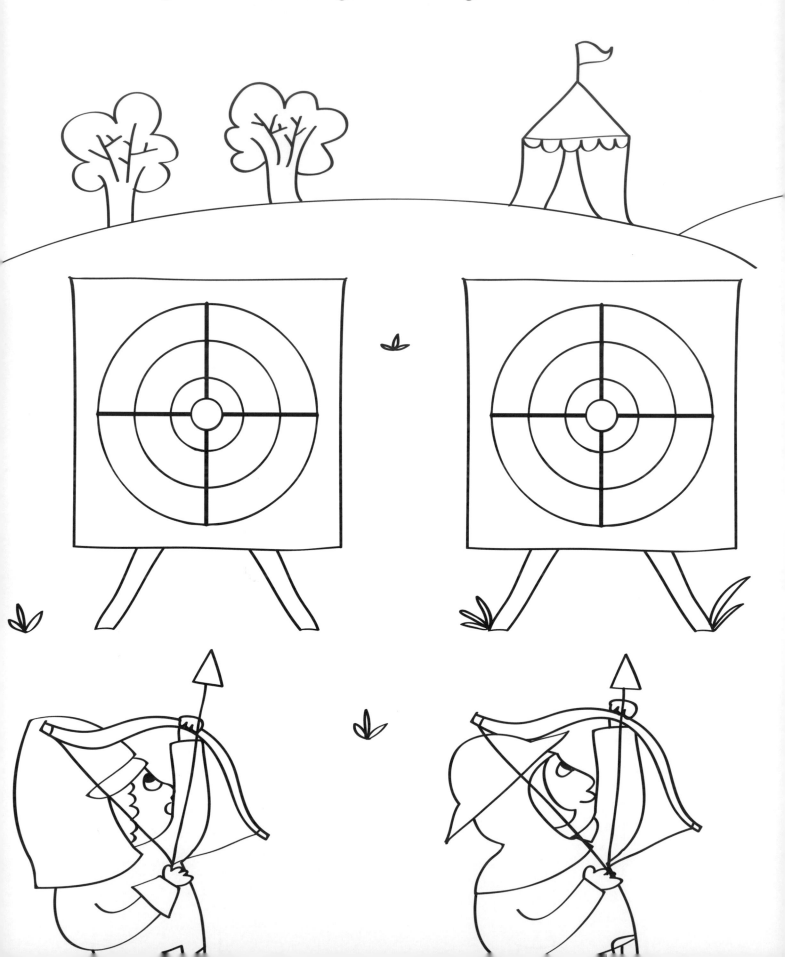

The royal artist is painting a picture. Draw something on her canvas.

The royal baker is baking something special.
Draw something in his oven.

Everyone in the kingdom is going to a masquerade ball.
Decorate these masks for them to wear.

Now draw a mask of your own!

Draw the other half of this throne!

Decorate and then color these beautiful cakes for the queen.

Now decorate and color these royal helmets for the king.

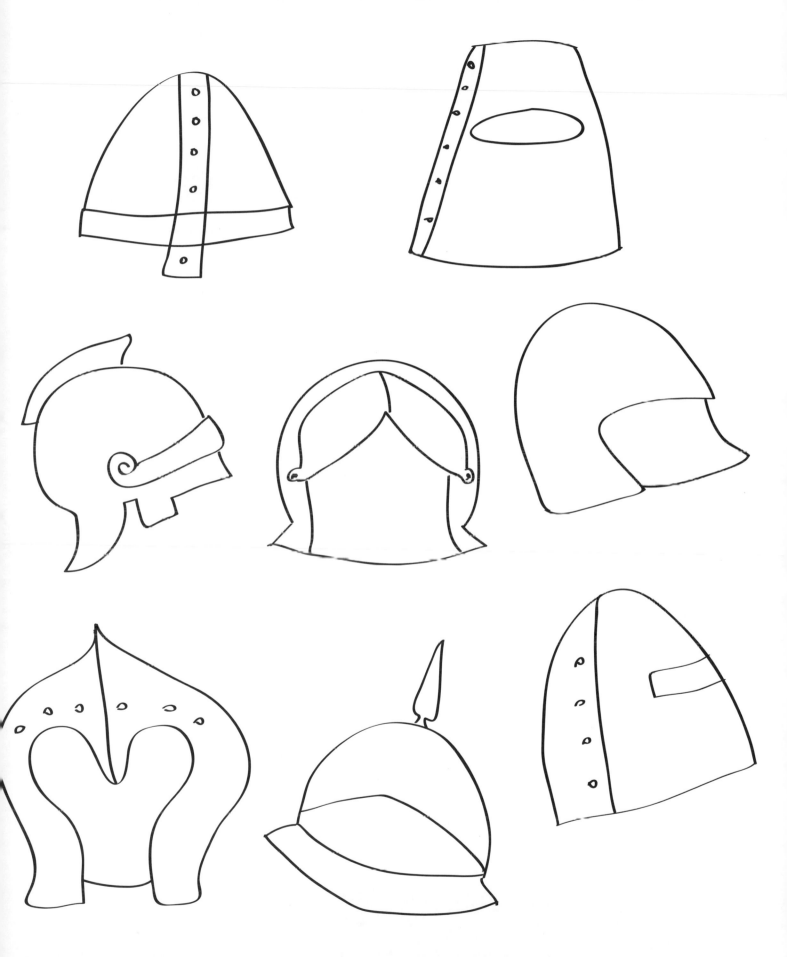

This wizard is about to turn this gnome into something else.
Color in the scene.

What does the gnome turn into? Draw it here!

Can you spot these images in the scene?

Fill these pages with a cool castle scene!

Color in this festive royal dancing scene!

A knight has lost his horse. Help the knight find his way to the horse.

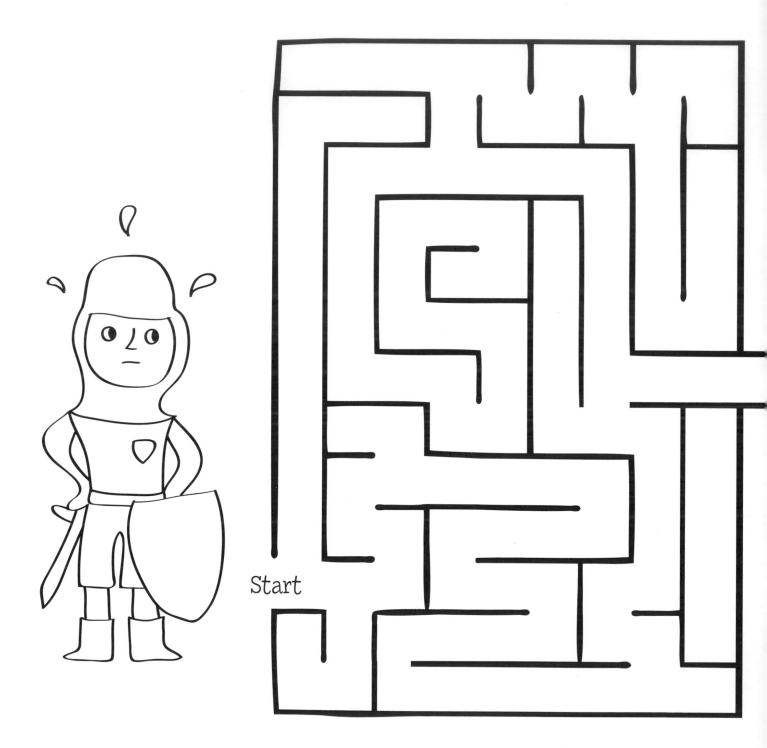

Start

Finish

There are many portraits in the portrait hall.
Draw some more inside the frames!

These guards are protecting a treasure chest.
Fill it with jewels, and color in the scene.

Welcome to the farm! Color in this scene.

These pigs are having some fun in the mud. Draw more pigs!

Can you spot all eight chickens in this scene?
Circle them and then color them in.

Add some more hay bales to make a pyramid.

What's inside the stable? Turn the page to find out.

Horses! Color them in.

Now color in the horses' saddles.

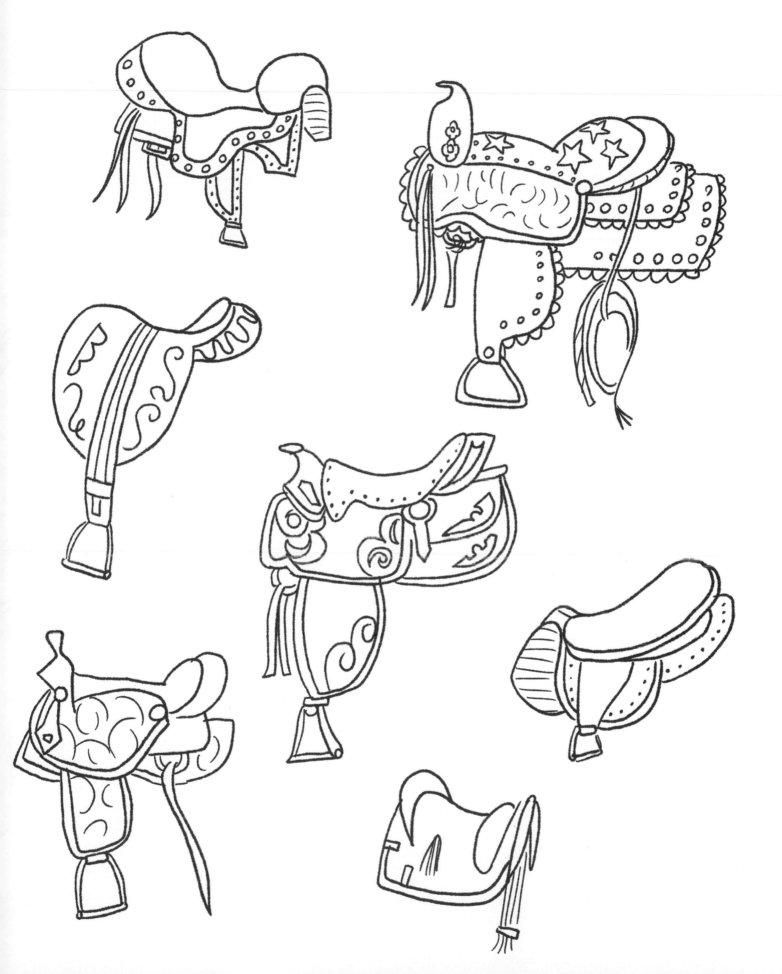

The farmer needs to get back to her barn. Can you help her?

Start

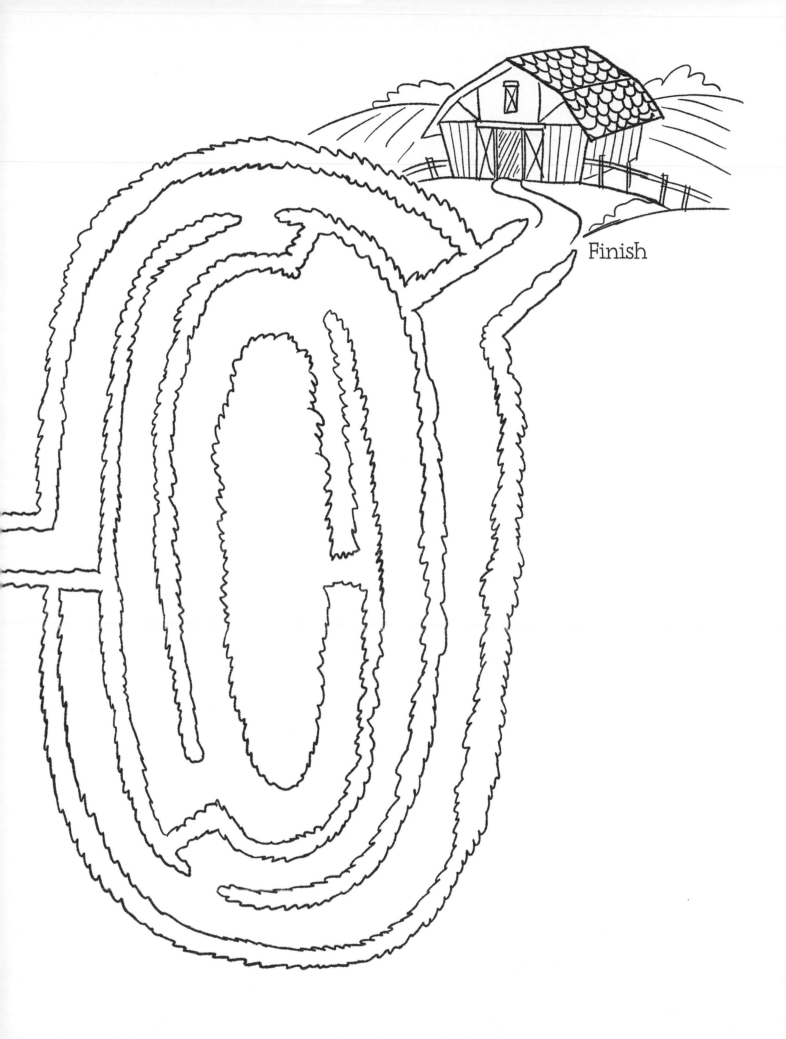

Finish

These are some of the animals on the farm. Color them in!

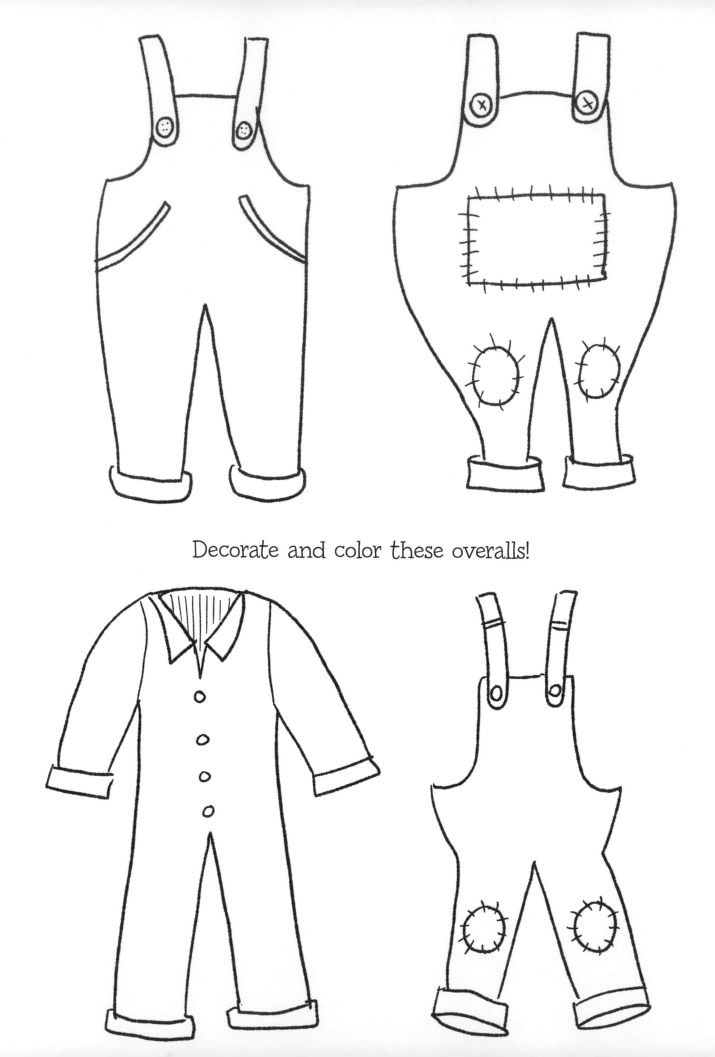

Decorate and color these overalls!

Connect the dots to see what's grazing in the field.

There's a beautiful flower field on the farm. Color in the flowers.

Now decorate this vase and add some flowers to the stems.

What is being pulled in the wheelbarrow? Draw it!

Let's get silly. Draw some sunglasses on these animals!

These birds need a place to perch. Draw a birdhouse for them!

It's time for some strawberry picking! Color in the scene.

Which two cows are exactly alike?

What is this farmer thinking about? Draw it in his thought bubble.

Doodle some designs on these hats.

This is the toolshed. Color in the tools.

The country road is long and winding.
Draw some cows in the fields on either side of the road.

Bees help pollinate the flowers.
Color in this scene and draw some more bees!

This scarecrow isn't very scary. Draw some more birds on him.

This piglet needs to find her mother.
Can you help her through the corn maze?

Start

Finish

Color in these apple trees.

Now color in this apple pie!

It's time for a hayride. Draw more people on the wagon!

These eggs are hatching!

The eggs have hatched. Look at the adorable baby chicks! Color them in and pick a name for each one. Write the names on the lines below.

Can you spot the eight ladybugs in this cornfield?

Match the animal to the sound it makes!

Neigh-Neigh

Cock-a-Doodle-Doo

Oink-Oink

Moo-Moo

This barn needs some
windows, doors, and decoration!

Color in these barns.

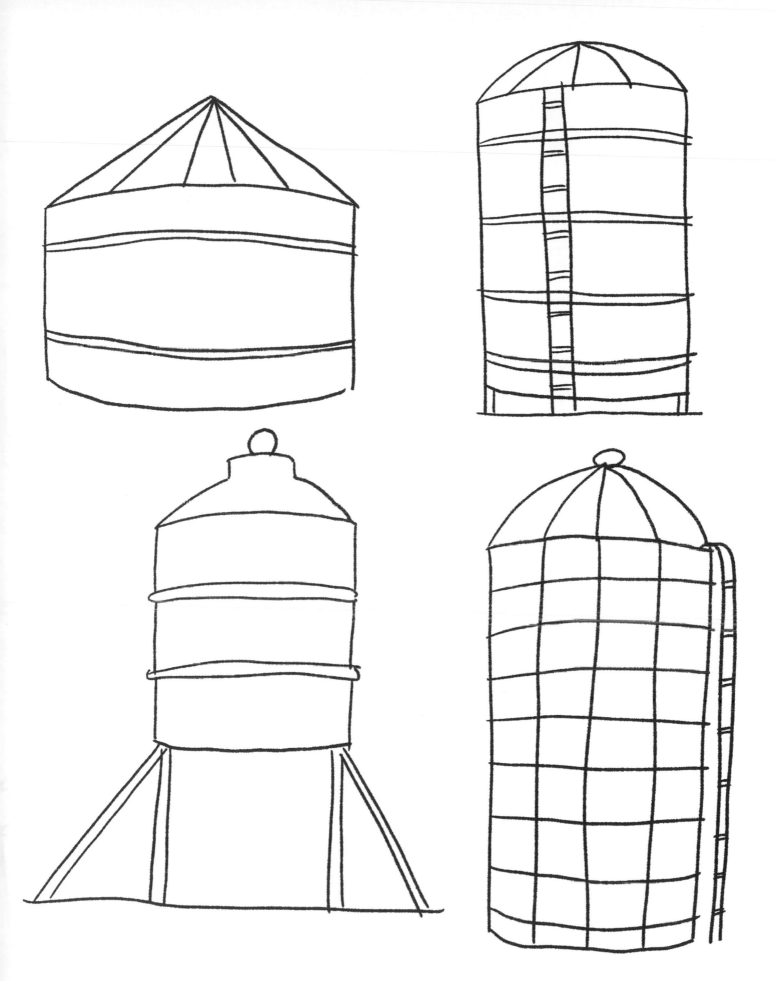

Now color in these silos.

Many vegetables grow in the ground.
Can you color the radishes red and the carrots orange?

Who's peeking out of these windows? Draw them!

This is the chicken coop. Draw some more chickens!

This is the sheep pen. Draw some more sheep!

The sun helps the fruit and vegetables on the farm grow.
Add a sun to the sky and color in the scene.

Draw the other half of this tree!

There's a big lake on the farm. Draw some fish in it!

Can you spot these images in the scene?

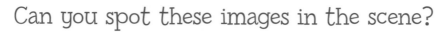

This is some of the machinery used on the farm.

Plow

Wagon

Ladder

Wheelbarrow

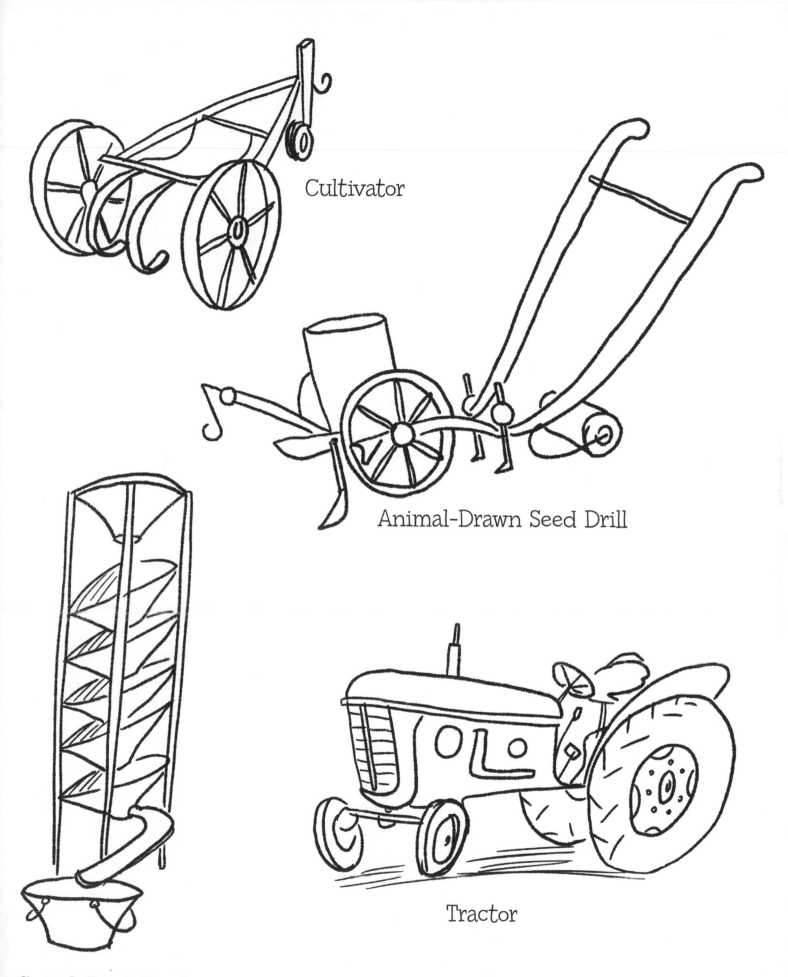

Cultivator

Animal-Drawn Seed Drill

Spiral Seed Grader

Tractor

Let's have some fun! Decorate these cows with
wacky stripes and polka dots.

Now do the same for these horses!

It's time for a tractor race! Which tractor do you think will win?
Draw it crossing the finish line.

Connect the dots to see a surprise!

The fruit on these pear trees is perfectly ripe.
Draw some more pears on the trees and in the buckets!

Using this chart, color each of these things
the opposite color from what it should be!

Opposites
Red & Green
Orange & Blue
Yellow & Purple
Black & White

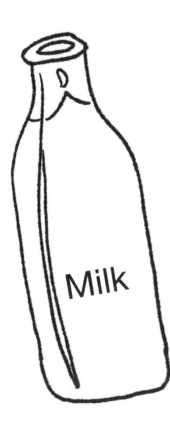

Milk

What does this farmer see out her window? Draw it.

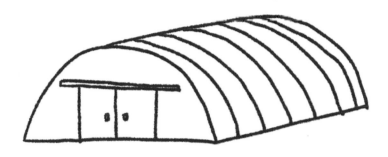

Look at all these barns. Can you find the two that are exactly alike?

Fill these pages with a fun scene!

This pig is looking for some lunch.

What do you think he wants to eat? Draw it here!

Fill these pages with a cool farm scene!

These wild turkeys are exploring the farm.

Draw your own turkey on this page by tracing your hand
and adding a face on the thumb!

Can you spot these images in the scene?

Look at this fun farm scene!

Color all the circles in the scene blue.
Then color all the squares red.
And color all the triangles green.

Color in this scene!

This farmer must get to his horse. Can you help him?

Start

Finish

Look at all these scarecrows.
Can you find the two that are exactly alike? Circle them!

What's in each of these baskets? Draw it!

Color in these baby animals.